AF575851

ITALY

Tracy Vonder Brink

TABLE OF CONTENTS

A Crabtree Seedlings Book

Crabtree Publishing
crabtreebooks.com

School-to-Home Support for Caregivers and Teachers

This book helps children grow by letting them practice reading. Here are a few guiding questions to help the reader with building his or her comprehension skills. Possible answers appear here in red.

Before Reading:

- What do I think this book is about?
  - *I think this book is about Italy.*
  - *I think this book is about the food people eat in Italy.*
- What do I want to learn about this topic?
  - *I want to learn about the geography of Italy.*
  - *I want to learn about art in Italy.*

During Reading:

- I wonder why...
  - *I wonder why the dome in Florence was built so large.*
  - *I wonder why people in Venice travel by boats on canals.*
- What have I learned so far?
  - *I have learned that pizza was invented in Naples.*
  - *I have learned that Rome is the capital of Italy.*

After Reading:

- What details did I learn about this topic?
  - *I have learned that the city of Pompeii was destroyed nearly 2,000 years ago.*
  - *I have learned that Italy is a peninsula.*
- Read the book again and look for the vocabulary words.
  - *I see the word **peninsula** on page 3, and the word **canals** on page 16. The other glossary words are on pages 22 and 23.*

Italy is a country.

It is in **Europe**.

Italy is a **peninsula.**

Rome is the **capital**.

The city is more than 2,000 years old.

Most people in Italy speak Italian.

The Colosseum is a famous place in Rome.

Romans watched games there a long time ago.

People also visit the Trevi Fountain in Rome.

Three very old streets meet where it sits.

CLEMENS XII · PONT · MAX ·
AQVAM VIRGINEM
COPIA ET SALVBRITATE COMMENDATAM
CVLTV MAGNIFICO ORNAVIT
ANNO DOMINI MDCCXXXV · PONTIF · VI ·
PERFECIT BENEDICTVS XIV · PON · MAX

Florence is in central Italy.

The Ponte Vecchio is its oldest bridge.

It is more than 600 years old.

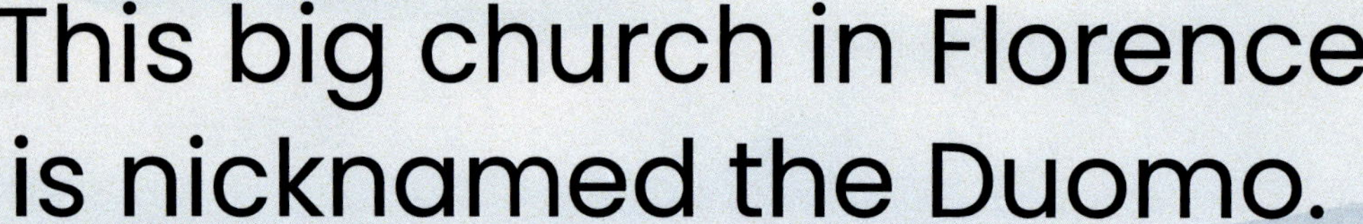

This big church in Florence is nicknamed the Duomo.

Its brick **dome** is the largest in the world.

The dome was built with more than 4 million bricks.

Pisa is also in central Italy.

Its tower is famous.

It leans because one side sank in soft ground.

Venice is in the North.

It has no roads for cars.

People travel by boat
on **canals**.

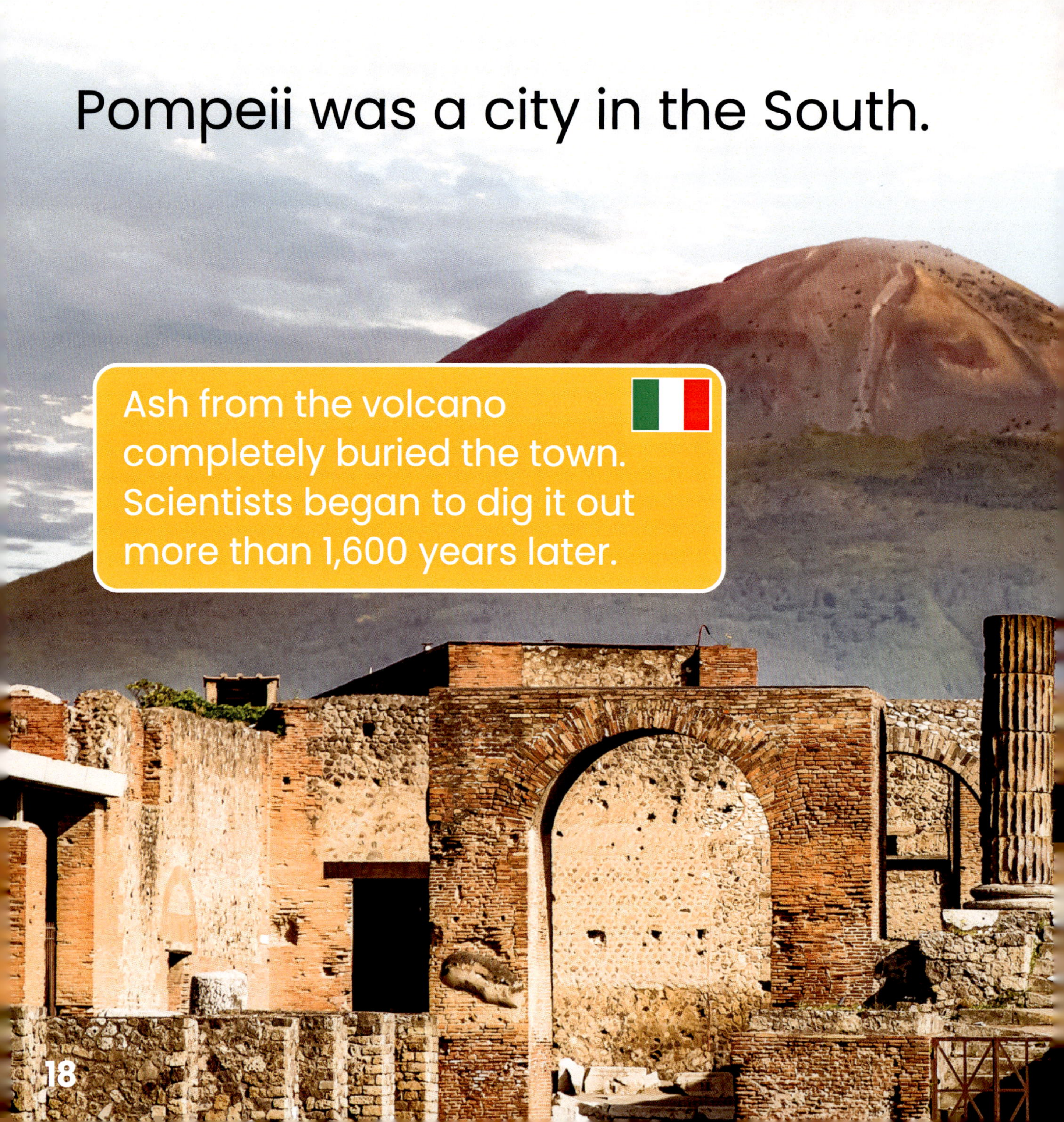

Pompeii was a city in the South.

Ash from the volcano completely buried the town. Scientists began to dig it out more than 1,600 years later.

A volcano destroyed it nearly 2,000 years ago.

Now, people visit its **ruins**.

Naples is also in the South.

Pizza was invented there.

Italy has many famous places!

Glossary

canal (kuh-NAL): A human-made waterway used to get boats from place to place or to bring water to farmland

capital (KAP-i-tl): The city where the government of a country or a state is located

dome (DOHM): A rounded roof or ceiling, shaped like half a ball

Europe (YOOR-up): The continent between the Atlantic Ocean and Asia

peninsula (puh-NIN-suh-luh): A piece of land mostly surrounded by water, but connected to a larger land area

ruins (ROO-unz): A city or buildings that have been destroyed

Index

About the Author

Tracy Vonder Brink

Tracy Vonder Brink loves to visit new places. She has been to Italy, and Venice was her favorite city there. She lives in Cincinnati with her husband, two daughters, and two rescue dogs.

Crabtree Publishing

crabtreebooks.com 800-387-7650

In Canada: We acknowledge the financial support of the Government of Canada through the Canada Book Fund for our publishing activities.

Hardcover 978-1-0396-4457-1
Paperback 978-1-0396-4648-3

Printed in the U.S.A./CP072026

Published in Canada
Crabtree Publishing
616 Welland Avenue
St. Catharines, Ontario
L2M 5V6

Published in the United States
Crabtree Publishing
347 Fifth Avenue
Suite 1402-145
New York, NY 10016

Written by: Tracy Vonder Brink
Print book version produced jointly with Blue Door Education in 2023
Production manager: Candice Campbell

Photo Credits: Shutterstock: Phant: cover; prosign: p. 3; Catarina Belova: p. 5; prochasson frederic: p. 7; beboy: p. 9; muratart: p. 11; Ralf Siemieniec: p. 12-13; Blue Planet Studio: p. 15; Efired: p. 17, 18-19; Seregan: p. 20; Bahdanovich Alena

Library and Archives Canada Cataloguing in Publication
Available at the Library and Archives Canada

Library of Congress Cataloging-in-Publication Data
Available at the Library of Congress